Charles Plumptre Johnson

The Early Writings of William Makepeace Thackeray

Charles Plumptre Johnson

The Early Writings of William Makepeace Thackeray

ISBN/EAN: 9783337219925

Printed in Europe, USA, Canada, Australia, Japan

Cover: Foto ©Andreas Hilbeck / pixelio.de

More available books at **www.hansebooks.com**

The Early Writings

OF

William Makepeace Thackeray

BY

CHARLES PLUMPTRE JOHNSON

*WITH ILLUSTRATIONS AFTER W. M. THACKERAY,
CHINNERY, F. WALKER AND R. DOYLE*

LONDON

ELLIOT STOCK, 62, PATERNOSTER ROW, E.C.

1888

Of this Book the following copies have been printed for sale :

1. On large paper 50
2. On hand-made paper 50
3. On antique paper 450
   ———
   550

TO

MRS. RICHMOND RITCHIE

IS

Dedicated

THIS ATTEMPT TO RECORD SOME OF

THE UNKNOWN EARLY WRITINGS

OF

HER GREAT FATHER

TABLE OF CONTENTS.

LIST OF ILLUSTRATIONS.

INTRODUCTION.

THE more ardent admirers of Thackeray and of his works are, for the most part, so far as regards the republication of his early and little-known writings, members of one or the other of two strongly opposed parties. The adherents of the one party stoutly assert that writings which the author did not himself collect and republish should be allowed to remain in the oblivion to which he, as they argue, deliberately consigned them, and from which it is, they say, inconsistent with a due regard to his wishes to rescue them. The members of the other party, with equal conviction, argue that every word which so great a writer ever gave to the world should be carefully searched for, and, when found, republished and carefully preserved for posterity.

The true and just course appears, as is usually the case, to be somewhere between those advocated by the extreme partisans on either side. Whatever interested persons may think proper to do for their own profit, it surely cannot be right that every unconsidered immature trifle from the pen of a great writer should be indiscriminately brought to light and issued broadcast to the general body of readers,

many of whom are sure to be ignorant of his greater
writings, are too likely to judge of his ability
from the first specimens of his work which they
meet, and may thus be led to do injustice to his
worth, and to lose the benefit they might otherwise
derive from studying his greater works. On the
other hand, it is not becoming for anybody to say
that the student, bibliographer and collector should
be debarred from reading, recording and possessing
even the most juvenile and trivial productions of a
great author. It is contended, then, that the proper
course is for those who find a pleasure in seeking
for and unearthing the early writings of great writers,
on the one hand, not selfishly to keep the results
of their labours to themselves, and, on the other, not
to publish them in a form likely to reach, or appeal
to, the general public, but to do what in them lies
to make their treasures known to others of similar
tastes, who may be expected to appreciate them.

This plan has been adopted as far as possible in
the case of these essays, which originally appeared
in *The Athenæum*, and are now collected and republished, with considerable alterations and additions.
The number of copies printed has been limited, and
the mode of publication has been chosen with the
express object of confining the circulation of these
notes to genuine and enthusiastic lovers and students
of Thackeray's works, who may be glad of any addi-
tion to their knowledge of his earlier writings, and
may be safely trusted not to misjudge his genius on
account of his ' small potatoes,' as he called his lesser
writings in conversation with Mr. James T. Fields
on the subject of similar republications. One other
explanation is needed. To the enthusiastic collector
nothing is more trying than to be told of writings

which are unquestionably *desiderata*, only to find
that they are also to be classed among *introuvables*.
To avoid, as far as possible, producing this result,
the unquestionable contributions by Thackeray to
the now practically unobtainable little periodicals,
The Snob and *The Gownsman*, have been here reprinted in the order in which they originally appeared. Of these writings the only one which is
included in the standard editions of Thackeray's
works is ' Timbuctoo,' far the best of them all,
which is here reprinted, so that the collection may
be as far as possible complete. It is hoped that the
possession of these reprinted papers may in some
degree tend to console those who are unable to find
the periodicals in which they originally appeared.

The fact that a mere collection of titles, dates
and references proves to all but the earnest bibliographer but dull reading, explains the occasional introduction among the notes of extracts from letters
and from the more interesting of the writings which
are here ascribed to Thackeray. Some readers, too,
may not care to wade through the pages of old
magazines and newspapers in search of all the articles
mentioned, and may be glad to have these extracts
as specimens of these early works.

It is scarcely necessary to state that these notes
have no claim to be considered complete, even as
regards the subjects of which they specially treat.
They are put forward merely as Essays in Bibliography, or, as they were originally called, ' Notes
and Queries for a Bibliography of the Writings of
W. M. Thackeray.'' They may, or may not lead to
identification of further writings, but all that is
claimed for them is that they identify beyond question many hitherto unrecognised writings of one of

the greatest of English authors, and that in every case the authority which is relied upon for such identification is duly quoted.

The illustrations can hardly fail to be of interest. Particulars of them are given in the 'List of Illustrations,' and need not be repeated here, but I have to express my thanks to Mrs. Richmond Ritchie for the very interesting portraits of her Father and of his Father and Mother; also to Dr. Julius Pollock, Mr. J. H. Round, and Mr. Frederick Chapman for the portraits and other illustrations, which I am enabled to give owing to their kindness.

C. P. J.

May 23rd, 1888.

THE EARLY WRITINGS

OF

WM. MAKEPEACE THACKERAY.

——◦——

CHAPTER I.

Irish Melody—*The Snob—The Gownsman—The Chimæra*—Essay on Shelley—At Weimar—Goethe—Schiller.

IN *Thackeray the Humourist and the Man of Letters*, which was published in 1864 by the late Mr. John Camden Hotten, and was in all probability written by him, though the title-page gives the author's name as 'Theodore Taylor, Esq.,' it is recorded (pp. 188-190) on the authority of Dr. Cornish, then vicar of Ottery St. Mary, near Exeter, that when Thackeray was staying there as a boy, he wrote and brought to Dr. Cornish some verses, which duly appeared in 'an Exeter paper.' Unfortunately no more information was given, and a diligent search among the files of the Exeter papers of the period has failed to bring the verses to light. They are, however, quoted in Mr. Hotten's book, and as they were in all probability the first writings of Thackeray to be published, they are worth repeating here :

I

'IRISH MELODY.

'AIR.—"The Minstrel Boy."

'Mister Sheil into Kent has gone,
    On Penenden Heath you'll find him;
Nor think you that he came alone,
    Here's Doctor Doyle behind him.
" Men of Kent," said this little man,
    " If you hate Emancipation,
You're a set of fools;" he then began
    A " cut and dry " oration.

' He strove to speak, but the men of Kent
    Began a grievous shouting,
When out of his waggon the little man went
    And put a stop to his spouting.
" What though those heretics heard me not,"
    Quoth he to his friend Canonical,
" My speech is safe in the *Times*, I wot,
    And eke in the *Morning Chronicle*." '

The first real attempt at literature on the part
of the future author of *Vanity Fair* and *Esmond*
was during his residence at Cambridge, in 1829,
when he appeared as one of the principal contributors to, and practically joint-editor of *The Snob*, a
little weekly periodical, eleven numbers of which
were published at Cambridge in 1829. He was probably not at first one of the most extensive writers
in *The Snob*, but the letters here quoted show that
the greater part of the work soon fell upon him. In a
letter dated the 17th May, 1829, Thackeray writes:
'A poem of mine hath appeared in a weekly periodical here published, and called *The Snob*. I will

bring it home with me.' And on a later day, but in
the same letter, he writes: ' " Timbuctoo " received
much laud. The men knew not the author, but
praised the poem.' This reference is, of course, to
Thackeray's burlesque lines on the subject given for
the prize poem, the prize being won by the present
Poet Laureate. The burlesque appeared in No. 4,
which was published on the 30th April, 1827. It
was reprinted, first in Hotten's book before referred
to, and again in the twenty-fifth volume of the
' Standard Edition ' of Thackeray's works, published
by Messrs. Smith and Elder in 1885. It is here
reprinted for the reasons given in the Introduction.

Criticism is beyond the scope of this volume, but
an expression of admiration of these verses may
perhaps be excused. They certainly indicate more
clearly than any other of Thackeray's juvenile efforts
the powers of humour then latent in their boyish
writer. The notes are by no means the least funny
part of the effusion.

' TIMBUCTOO.

' *To the Editor of " The Snob."*

' SIR,—Though your name be " Snob," I trust you
will not refuse this tiny " Poem of a Gownsman,"
which was unluckily not finished on the day ap-
pointed for delivery of the several copies of verses
on Timbuctoo. I thought, sir, it would be a pity
that such a poem should be lost to the world ; and
conceiving " The Snob " to be the most widely circu-
lated periodical in Europe, I have taken the liberty
of submitting it for insertion or approbation.

' I am, sir, yours, etc., etc., etc.,

' T.'

'TIMBUCTOO.—PART I.

The situation.—In Africa (a quarter of the world)
Men's skins are black, their hair is crisp and curl'd ;
And somewhere there, unknown to public view,
A mighty city lies, called Timbuctoo.

The natural history.—There stalks the tiger,—there
    the lion roars,   5
Who sometimes eats the luckless blackamoors ;
All that he leaves of them the monster throws
To jackals, vultures, dogs, cats, kites, and crows ;
His hunger thus the forest monarch gluts,
And then lies down 'neath trees called cocoa nuts.   10

The lion hunt.—Quick issue out, with musket, torch
    and brand,
The sturdy blackamoors, a dusky band !

Lines 1 and 2.—See Guthrie's Geography :—
  The site of Timbuctoo is doubtful ; the Author has neatly expressed
this in the poem, at the same time giving us some slight hints relative to
its situation.
  Line 5.—So Horace—' *leonum arida nutrix.*'
  Line 8.—Thus Apollo :

$$\text{ἐλώρια τεύχε κύνεσσιν}$$
$$\text{Οἰωνοῖσι τε πᾶσι}$$

  Lines 5-10.—How skilfully introduced are the animal and vegetable
productions of Africa ! It is worthy to remark the various garments
in which the Poet hath clothed the Lion. He is called, 1st, the
Lion ; 2nd, the Monster, (for he is very large) ; and 3rd, the Forest
Monarch, which undoubtedly he is.
  Lines 11-14.—The author confesses himself under peculiar obliga-
tions to Denham's and Clapperton's Travels, as they suggested to him
the spirited description contained in these lines.

The beast is found—pop goes the musketoons—
The lion falls, covered with horrid wounds.

> *Their lives at home.*—At home their lives in pleasure
> always flow, 15
> But many have a different lot to know!
> *Abroad.*—They're often caught, and sold as slaves,
> alas!

Reflections on the foregoing.—Thus men from highest
joys to sorrow pass.
Yet though thy monarchs and thy nobles boil
Rack and molasses in Jamaica's isle? 20
Desolate Afric! thou art lovely yet!!
One heart yet beats which ne'er shall thee forget.
What though thy maidens are a blackish brown,
Does virtue dwell in whiter breasts alone?
Oh no, oh no, oh no, oh no, oh no! 25
It shall not, must not, cannot, e'er be so.

Line 13.—"Pop goes the musketoons." A learned friend suggested
"Bang" as a stronger expression, but as African gunpowder is noto.
riously bad, the Author thought "Pop" the better word.

Lines 15-18.—A concise but affecting description is here given of the
domestic habits of the people,—the infamous manner in which they are
entrapped and sold as slaves is described,—and the whole ends with an
appropriate moral sentiment. The Poem might here finish, but the
spirit of the bard penetrates the veil of futurity, and from it cuts off a
bright piece for the hitherto unfortunate Africans, as the following
beautiful lines amply exemplify.

It may perhaps be remarked that the Author has here "changed his
hand;" he answers that it was his intention to do so. Before, it was
his endeavour to be elegant and concise; it is now his wish to be enthusiastic and magnificent. He trusts the Reader will perceive the aptness
with which he hath changed his style; when he narrated facts he was
calm, when he enters on prophecy he is fervid.

The enthusiasm which he feels is beautifully expressed in lines 25-
26. He thinks he has very successfully imitated in the last six lines the
best manner of Mr. Pope; and in lines 12-26, the pathetic elegance of
the Author of 'Australasia and Athens.'

The day shall come when Albion's self shall feel
Stern Afric's wrath, and writhe 'neath Afric's steel.
I see her tribes the hill of glory mount,
And sell their sugars on their own account ;   30
While round her throne the prostrate nations come,
Sue for her rice, and barter for her rum !   32

In a letter written during May, 1829, Thackeray
says : 'I think after the vacation we shall set up
a respectable periodical here. I shall have four
months to write for it !' This reference was to *The
Gownsman*, the successor of *The Snob;* but his other
contributions to *The Snob* have still to be dealt with.

An undated letter says : 'I have put "Genevieve"
into it, *The Snob*, with a little alteration.' This
enables us to identify the following verses, which
appeared in No. 6, published on the 14th May, 1829.

' The Author cannot conclude without declaring that his aim in writing
this Poem will be fully accomplished, if he can infuse into the breasts
of Englishmen a sense of the danger in which they lie. Yes—Africa !
If he can awaken one particle of sympathy for thy sorrows, of love for
thy land, of admiration for thy virtue, he shall sink into the grave with
the proud consciousness that he has raised esteem, where before there
was contempt, and has kindled the flame of hope on the mouldering
ashes of Despair !'

'To Genevieve.

'A DISINTERESTED EPISTLE.

'Say do I seek, my Genevieve !
Thy charms alone to win ?
Oh, no ! for thou art fifty-five,
And uglier than sin !

'Or do I love the flowing verse
Upon thy syren tongue ?
Oh, no ! those strains of thine are worse
Than ever screech-owl sung.

'Since then I thus refuse my love
For songs or charms to give,
What could my tardy passion move ?
Thy money, Genevieve !

'A Literary Snob.'

On the 23rd May, 1829, he wrote : 'On Monday
night myself and the editor of *The Snob* sat down to
write *The Snob* for next Thursday. We began at
nine and finished at two ; but I was so afflicted with
laughter during our attempts that I came away quite
ill.' From this it would appear that Thackeray had
a large part in producing No. 8, for the 30th May,
1829.

Under date May 29 we read : '*The Snob* goeth on
and prospereth. Here is a specimen of my wit, in
the shape of an advertisement therein inserted :
"Sidney Sussex College.—Wanted, a few freshmen.
Apply at the Butteries, where the smallest contributions will be thankfully received." '

It has generally been considered, owing to the

peculiar orthography adopted in them, that the
'Ramsbottom Papers' were from Thackeray's pen.
This is more than probable, but as there is no actual
proof, they are not here reprinted.

One more suggestion and we have done with *The
Snob.* In the interesting letter printed in the
Athenæum of the 7th August, 1886, with reference to
Thackeray's 'Paris Sketch-Book,' it is recorded that
the letters written from Paris to the *Corsair* in 1839
were all signed 'T. T.' Now, Thackeray had a
curious liking for returning to the use of a former
nom de guerre, and this lends force to the suggestion
that he may have been responsible for a rhyming
letter published in the third number of *The Snob*
above the signature 'T. T.' This signature was
adopted by Thackeray in his Paris correspondence
for the ill-fated *Constitutional,* and though actual
proof of his authorship is lacking, the evidence seems
strong enough to justify the verses being printed
here to enable each to judge for himself on the
subject :

'EXTRACT FROM A LETTER, FROM ONE IN CAM-
BRIDGE, TO ONE IN TOWN.

'Of the Musical Clubs I shall say but a word,
  Since to none but the Members they pleasure
    afford.
The ——— still play as they usually did,
While the good-natured visitors praise what
    they're bid.
This law 'mid these sons of Apollo will tell :
"To play very loud, is to play very well ;"—
A concert "*piano*" they deem quite absurd,—
In music like that ev'ry blunder is heard ;

The best singer that Cambridge e'er saw, they
    agree,
Was a friend of my own that could reach reach
    double B ;
In fine, I imagine, they think it a crime
To spare any sound, or to lose any time,
So the laurels of course are by him always won,
Who makes the most noise, and who soonest cries
    " Done !"
Well enough of the —— ; The —— comes next,
" *Vox et praeterea nil* " is it's text ;
For though on it's list it still must be confest,
That of all Cambridge singers it numbers the
    best ;
Yet while, thro' good-nature, it falsely permits,
While the rest sing "*piano*," one screaming in fits,
It cannot expect unconditional praise,
Or more than politeness [one] to amateurs pays.
A word of the ——, and I've done—
They have but one fault, and a laughable one,
When seated at supper, they seem to forget
The purpose for which they pretend to have
    met ;
I was taken there once, and I found that good
    eating
Was the greatest if not the sole cause of their
    meeting.

                    T. T.'

In November, 1830, an effort was made to carry
out Thackeray's proposal in the letter before printed,
to 'set up a respectable periodical here.' In due
course *The Gownsman* made its appearance. It is
very difficult to estimate the nature and extent of
Thackeray's connection with this little paper. It

seems more than probable that he was actually editor, and had a large part in writing it. Until quite lately, however, no contribution of his was distinctly recognised. The scarceness of the paper may, to some extent, have accounted for this. There is no copy in the British Museum, and a copy of the title-page is accordingly given here. Such copies as come into the market from time to time usually lack the first number, from which we may perhaps conclude that the little periodical was, for a time, more successful than had been expected, and that a larger edition of the later numbers was issued. The full title of *The Gownsman* is as follows:

' THE GOWNSMAN, | (formerly called) " THE SNOB," | A Literary and Scientific Journal, | now | conducted by Members of the University.' | SIR,— Here is newly come to Court, Laertes; believe me an absolute | gentleman, full of most excellent differences. | HAMLET. | ' Vol. 2. | Cambridge : | Published by W. H. Smith, Rose Crescent | And sold by Simpkin and Marshall, London, | and may be had of all booksellers. | 1830.'

It is stated on the authority of Mr. Edward Fitz-gerald, who was a great friend of Thackeray's, that his contributions to *The Gownsman* were signed ' Θ,' a signature which he afterwards used for his famous article on his friend George Cruikshank, which appeared in the *Westminster Review* in 1840. This, if conceded, at once identifies Thackeray's writings for *The Gownsman*. The principal contribution so signed is a parody of ' I'd be a Butterfly,' and, curiously enough, shortly after the ascription to Thackeray of the ' Θ ' articles had been made in the *Athenæum*, a version of this parody, varying but slightly from the

published verses, and in his own handwriting, was
brought to light, having been found in an album
of autographs. The proof seems conclusive, and
another poem signed ' Θ ' is accordingly reprinted
here. The printed version of 'I'd be a Tadpole'
appeared in No. 2 of *The Gownsman* as follows :

' MODERN SONGS.—NO. 5.

' AIR.—" *I'd be a Butterfly.*"

' I'd be a tadpole, born in a puddle,
    Where dead cats, and drains, and water rats
       meet ;
There under a stone I so snugly would cuddle,
    With some other tad which was pretty and
       sweet.
I'd never seek my poor brains for to muddle
    With thinking why I had no toes to my feet ;
But under a stone I so snugly would cuddle
    With some other tad as was pretty and sweet.

' If I could borrow the wand of a fairy,
    I'd be a fish and have beautiful fins—
But yet in this puddle I'm cleanly and airy,
    I'm washed by the waters and cool'd by the
      winds !
Fish in a pond must be watchful and wary,
    Or boys will catch them with worms and hooked
      pins.
I'll be a tadpole, cleanly and airy,
    Washed by the waters and wiped by the winds.

' What though you tell me each black little rover
    Dies in the sun when the puddle is dry,—
Do you not think that when it's all over
    With my best friends I'll be happy to die ?

Some may turn toads with great speckled bellies,
　　Swim in the gutter, or spit on the road;
I'll stay a tadpole, and not like them fellers
　　Be one day a tad and the other a toad!

　　　　　　　　　　　　　　　　　Θ.'

The MS. version is as follows:

　　　　　'I'D BE A TADPOLE.

'I'd be a Tadpole, born in a puddle,
　　Where drowned dogs and kittens and water-rats
　　　　meet;
And under a stone I so snugly would cuddle,
　　With some other tad that was pretty and
　　　　sweet.
I'd never seek my poor brains for to muddle
　　With thinking why I had no toes to my feet;
But under a stone I so snugly would cuddle
　　With some other tad as was pretty and sweet.

'Oh, could I borrow the wand of a fairy,
　　I'd be a fish and have beautiful fins!
Yet in my puddle I'm cleanly and airy,　　　.
　　I'm washed by the waters and dried by the
　　　　winds.
Fish in a pond must be watchful and wary,
　　Or boys will catch them with worms and hooked
　　　　pins!
So I'll be a tadpole, cleanly and airy,
　　Washed by the waters and wiped by the winds.

'Sad tho' the fate of each black little rover
　　When summer comes, and the puddle gets dry—
Why, my good friends, when our fun is all over,
　　Is it not better for tadpoles to die?

Some may turn toads, and with great speckled
  bellies,
Swim in the gutter, or crawl in the road;
I'll die a tadpole! and not like them fellies
Be one day a tad and the other a toad!

The following lines appeared in No. 5:

'FROM ANACREON.

'Prepare thy silver, god of fire,
  And light thy forges up;
No soldier I to ask of thee
Bright arms and glittering panoply;
To these let warrior chiefs aspire—
  I ask a mighty cup!

'A mighty cup! but draw not on it
  Orion grim with clubs advancing,
Or heavenly wains, or rampant bears;
What cares Anacreon for the stars?
Draw Love and my Bathyllus on it,
  Mid clustering vines with Bacchus dancing.
                                    Θ.'

These are the only papers which can with certainty be attributed to Thackeray, though the
'Ramsbottom Papers,' continued from *The Snob*,
and many other writings, were probably by him, and
Anthony Trollope suggested that the dedication 'To
all Proctors,' etc., was probably written by Thackeray.
  In the latter part of the year 1829 Thackeray was
in Paris, and was there engaged in writing 'An
Essay on Shelley' for the *Chimæra*, a magazine
published, or intended to be published, at Cambridge. The magazine cannot be found in the
British Museum, but, if anybody has access to a

copy, he should search through the numbers for the latter part of 1829 and the beginning of 1830 for any essay on the subject. Thackeray proposed to use as a motto for his article a quotation from Lord Lytton's novel 'Devereux,' which may serve to identify his work if it was published in the *Chimæra* or elsewhere. The interest of such an essay from Thackeray's pen would be great.

Though somewhat beyond the plan and intention of these notes, a few passages from some of Thackeray's letters written at Weimar in 1830, bearing upon his literary pursuits, ideas, and occupations, are here quoted. It will be remembered that at this time he was a Cambridge undergraduate, aged nineteen :

'Wednesday, *October* 20, 1830.

' I saw for the first time old Goethe to-day; he was very kind, and received me in rather a more *distingué* manner than he has used the other Englishmen here ; the old man gives occasionally a tea-party, to which the English and some special favourites in the town are invited ; he sent me a summons this morning to come to him at twelve. I sat with him for half an hour, and took my leave on the arrival of ——.'

Again :

' Madame de Goethe was "very kind." . . . When I went to call on her, I found her with three *Byrons*, a *Moore*, and a *Shelley* on her table.'

As we read, we wonder whether the shrewd old German, then approaching the end of his life, and having done his work, saw anything specially remarkable about the big English boy who, with so many others, went to worship at his shrine.

On the 17th November, 1830, Thackeray writes, still from Weimar :

' I have read " Faust," with which, of course, I am delighted, but not to that degree I expected.'

He suggests, in a letter of the 4th December, 1830, the idea of obtaining an attachéship and settling down at Weimar. The world may indeed be congratulated that this suggestion was not carried out.

The most interesting of these letters from Weimar runs as follows :

' *February* 25, 1831.

' Talking of Schiller, I am in possession of his handwriting and of his veritable court sword, and I do believe him to be, after Shakespeare, " the Poet." . . . I have been reading Shakespeare in German. If I could ever do the same for Schiller in English, I should be proud of having conferred a benefit on my country !'

It is said that during his stay at Weimar, where he made many friends, Thackeray contributed both with pencil and pen to the albums of several of the young ladies there. We may hope that some of these young ladies are still living, though no longer young, and that they have preserved their albums to hand down to their children's children.

During the year 1831 Thackeray appears to have seriously studied for the bar, as letters of this period show ; for instance :

' In Mr. Taprell's Chambers, Hare Court, Temple,
'*December* 16, 1831.

' I have just finished a long-winded declaration about a mortgage.'

Solicitors who sent papers to Mr. Taprell about this time might, as a matter of curiosity, institute a search for the ' long-winded declaration ' in question, or other similar documents, in the beautifully neat writing of the pupil, and, in all probability, ruthlessly cut about and ' settled ' by his master.

In January, 1833, a letter is written from ' 5, Essex Court,' Temple, where Thackeray appears to have been then living. We may suppose that it was during this period of his life that he acquired that knowledge of the habits of dwellers in chambers in the Temple which he turned to such good account in *Pendennis* and other of his writings.

2

T.

CHAPTER II.

As is well known, Thackeray's residence at Cambridge did not last long, and after his subsequent
stay in Germany he went to Paris and studied art
more or less assiduously. He appears, however, to
have had an irresistible yearning for writing and for
journalism, which was destined first to bring him
loss and trouble, then gain and fame.

In the years 1831 and 1832 Mr. F. W. N. Bayley, a
prolific contributor to the serial publications of the
day, was engaged in editing and writing for *The
National Omnibus.* Thackeray was unquestionably
acquainted with Bayley, but whether he contributed
anything to *The National Omnibus* is uncertain, though
some sketches of literary men of the day which appeared there might well have come from his pencil,
and some of the verses are not at all unlike his early
work. *The National Omnibus* was at first issued
' gratis '; this not proving profitable, its price was
put at ' one penny.' It not unnaturally failed, and
from its ashes rose *The National Standard and Journal
of Literature, Science, Music, Theatricals, and the Fine
Arts,* the first number of which appeared on the 5th
January, 1833. It was a weekly journal, ' edited by

2—2

F. W. N. Bayley, Esq.,' and sold for twopence.
Very early in its career Thackeray became a contributor. He certainly was the author of the verses
on Louis Philippe which appeared with a sketch
in the eighteenth number. With the nineteenth
number Thackeray seems to have assumed the
editorship, and the address at the beginning of that
number was no doubt written by him.

Dr. John Brown, in the *North British Review* for
July, 1864, expressed his opinion that Thackeray
with this number became editor; and it will be seen
from the letters quoted below that he also became
the owner of the paper, and that the articles written
by him must have been far more numerous than has
hitherto been supposed.

The first letter we have to quote is as follows :

'Meurice's, Rue Rivoli, *July* 6, 1833.

'About all I have seen I refer you to *The National
Standard*, to which I have written a great letter this
morning.'

This is the only letter we can quote which refers to
the Paris correspondence, but these contributions
are easily recognisable as Thackeray's work. In the
'Bibliography' appended to Mr. Shepherd's edition
of 'Sultan Stork' (where some of these Paris letters
and some verses from the same pen are reprinted) it
is stated that with the number for the 24th August,
1833 (in which 'The Devil's Wager' appeared),
'Thackeray's contributions appear to have ceased';
but this was not the case, as is shown by the following letters referring to later work for *The National
Standard :*

'Garrick Club, *September* 6, 1833.

'I must stay for some time longer, being occupied in writing, puffing, and other delightful occupations for the *N. Standard.* . . . *The National Standard* is, I am glad to say, growing into repute, though I know it is poor stuff.'

Whatever the author may have thought, he would probably find few people to agree with him in his criticism.   Surely it was no small thing at the age of twenty-two, probably with but little help from others, to have conducted and kept alive for more than a year a journal treating of such varied subjects as did *The National Standard*, and treating of them in a manner by no means to be despised.   The volumes themselves are very difficult to get, but an inspection of them will well repay a visit to the British Museum, not only for the letterpress, but also for the quaint woodcuts, some of which show the touch of the true humourist as strongly as do the best of Thackeray's later efforts in the art of illustration.

On the 7th September, 1833, under the heading of 'Foreign Literature,' appeared a short note, signed 'W.,' to which were appended first some verses in *patois*, then a translation.   There can be little doubt as to the authorship of the verses, which are an early example of the fondness that Thackeray showed sometimes in after-life for introducing a touch of burlesque in a seemingly incongruous manner.

On the 23rd October, 1833, Thackeray was in Paris again, and wrote as follows:

'I admire your indignation about the old woman and the sack of beans.   It is translated from a very clever French story, which is written in a sort of *patois*.   I suppose I have not imitated it well, for I sent away the performance the day it was written, and one does not know good from bad then. I have sent nothing else, except a cheque, but the paper is very rapidly improving, and will form, I have no doubt, a property, in which case it would be pleasant as an occupation and an income.'

This letter refers to an article which appeared in the number for the 12th October, 1833, under the title of ' Original Papers : A Tale of Wonder,' and is worthy of preservation as a good specimen of Thackeray's early prose style. We therefore give it here :

' ORIGINAL PAPERS.

' A TALE OF WONDER.

' Once upon a time there was an old woman who lived in a village not far off, and who went to market to buy a sack of beans. Now she had to walk back ten miles over a dreary common ; a long step at most times, but a terrible pull when one has a sack of beans on one's back. It was night before she got half way, and the moon was hid, and the snow was falling, and the old woman was ready to drop ; she was tired and hungry ; so she was right glad when she came to a house, which, though an ugly-looking place at the best, she thought quite good enough for her to rest in.

' She took out a penny, and asked for a bed, and the woman of the house let her go into a loft, where she slept on her sack of beans.

' Now the house belonged to thieves; and this was one of their wives who let in the woman with her sack.

' But, though the old woman was so tired, she could not sleep, but lay tossing about on her straw quite uneasy: presently she saw a light in the room below, and two men, each with a knife and a lantern.

'And she felt desperately frightened, as you may fancy, for she thought they might want to murder her, and then eat her, which was often done in those days, when there were a great many ogres and giants.

'Well, the two men with the knives went on till they came to a bed where a gentleman was sleeping, who had been overtaken like the old woman, and who had got with him a large portmanteau; there he lay as sound as possible, snoring away in a manner quite pleasant to hear. As soon as the two rogues saw how fast asleep he was, the biggest took hold of his legs, and the little one took out his knife and cut the gentleman's throat, slick! at one slash.

'As soon as they had stuck him they left him there all bloody, took the portmanteau and went away again downstairs: the old woman with the sack became mighty uneasy, thinking that it was to be her turn next, and that it was all over with her for certain; whereas Heaven had sent her there on purpose to detect and punish these wicked men. As soon as they got downstairs, the woman must have told them of the poor old creature in the loft, for presently up they came again, knives and lanterns and all.

'The poor old body was terribly frightened, as you may think, especially when the big man took hold of her legs (as he had done below stairs), and the little one came up to her head, with his lantern and his long knife.

'However, she did not move a muscle, only she snored to make believe she was asleep.

'"Let's leave her," says the big man; "she's asleep and can tell no tales."

' " Let's *kill her*," says the little one ; "she'll do to feed the pigs !"

' All this while the old woman lay as still as a stone ; and, at last, as they did not suspect that she was awake, they let her off, and went downstairs. So she escaped like a brave old woman as she was ! She saw them wrap up the dead man below in his sheet and carry him to the courtyard ; presently they called the pigs, and up they came, grunting and snuffling round the trough, which was the coffin that these wicked monsters gave the poor murdered gentleman.

' You may suppose that she did not sleep much that night, but the next morning, as soon as it was light, she thanked the woman of the house, took up her sack, and set off home as though nothing had happened ; trudging over the common as fast as her poor legs would carry her, though that was not very fast, she trembled so. Now the little man (he that had stuck the gentleman) suspected that all was not right, and he followed her, and came up with her before she had got a mile on the road. As soon as she saw him coming, the bold old lady puts down her sack, and sits waiting for him on a stone.

' " What's the matter, missus ?" says he.

' " Why, my sack is heavy, and my old legs is rather weak ; I wish some honest man would give me an arm, and help me on my road a bit."

' So the little fellow gave her his arm ; and there they went across the common, talking about beans, and the weather, and what not, as if they had been two angels. He saw her almost home ; and you may be sure that when she got there she fell down on her knees and said her prayers ; as well she might, after getting off so well.

' While she was in the middle of her prayers, in

comes her husband; and as soon as she'd done, he asked for a bit of bacon and some of the beans; so she cut a large piece, and plenty of beans. While it was boiling she told her husband of all she had seen the night before.

'"I must go to the Justice," says she, "and tell him the whole story."

'"Go to the Justice, go the devil," says he; "as for the gentleman, it is all over with him now, and some of these rogues' comrades will kill us if we peach."

'With that, he stuck his fork into the saucepan to catch hold of a bit of the bacon. Well, as sure as I'm sitting here, instead of pulling out a bit of pork, what does he find at the end of his fork but a man's head!

'"It's the gentleman's head," said the wife.

'"But what can we do?" says her husband, who was rather flustered.

'"You can revenge me!" says the head. "Last night I was wickedly murdered, and eaten by pigs, as your wife can swear to. I shall have no rest until I see those robbers at the gallows; and what's more, I'll never leave you till then!"

'So the farmer told the Justice, and the thieves were hanged, and all the pigs drowned who had eaten the gentleman's body.

'"And the head?"

'Why, it was buried in the field where the farmer sowed the beans, and there was never such crops known as came from that field.

'"And the brave old woman?"

'Why, though she was seventy years old, she had a son, and lived happy ever after.'

The identification of this paper leads us to suppose that several of the 'Original Papers,' published about

this time in *The National Standard*, may have been
written by Thackeray; but I hesitate to attribute
them to him without some unquestionable evidence.
The curious in such matters may, however, be recom-
mended to read 'The History of Crakatuk,' which
will be found in the numbers for the 30th November
and the 7th December, 1833. The story is a translation from the German and shows unmistakable signs
of skill.

The following letter is interesting as showing at
once the progress the paper made, and its owner's
trials and anxiety:

'Garrick Club, *Tuesday, November* 12, 1833.

' My *National Standard* as usual! It has increased
in sale about twenty in the last month. At this rate
I shall be ruined before it succeeds.'

The varied nature and the extent of the unfortunate editor's labours are clearly set out here:

'*December* 23, 1833.

' The only fault I find with *The National Standard*
is that at the end of the day I am but ill-disposed,
after writing and reading so much, to read another
syllable or write another line. . . . I am anxious the
first number for the new year should be a particu-
larly good one, as I am going to change the name
to *The Literary Standard*, and increase the price to
threepence, with which alterations I hope to do
better.'

In due course, at the beginning of the year, *The
National Standard* appeared with an altered title,
though not that proposed in the last letter. The
new name was *The National Standard and Literary*

Representative. Its price was threepence; and a most confident address in the last number for 1833 heralded its future doings and expected success. Among the contents were to be (doubtless from the editor's pen) translations from the German and other foreign languages. Two such translations appeared, ' King Odo's Wedding,' and ' The Minstrel's Curse,' when a sudden collapse came, and, without any notice to its readers, the publication of *The National Standard* ended abruptly with the number for the 1st February, 1834.

I must not conclude these references to *The National Standard* without mentioning the following points. In the number for the 18th January, 1834, appeared a piece of Irish fun, called ' Father Gahagan's Exhortation.' Here we have Thackeray's first use of the name ' Gahagan,' which afterwards became well known to his readers. Again, the signature Θ crops up in the last numbers. First we find it under a short paragraph in the last number but one; and a long article, entitled ' Étude sur Mirabeau, par Victor Hugo,' in the last number, is also signed Θ.

CHAPTER III.

THE actual facts as to Thackeray's connection with
The Constitutional are almost, if not quite, unknown,
and are, at all events, unrecorded. His associations
with *The National Standard* and *The Constitutional*
have often been confused the one with the other,
and it has been supposed that his financial ruin was
caused by the former, whereas it is clear enough that
it was the attempt to rival the old-established daily
papers with *The Constitutional* that impoverished the
youthful Thackeray, and consequently enriched our
literature with some of its brightest ornaments. The
heavy expenditure involved in the production of a
journal such as *The Constitutional* may be gathered
from the following contemporary estimate of the
profits *expected* from its publication :

No. 2.

State of Receipts and Disbursements with 1,000 addl :

Dr.		Cr.			
Weekly expenses = 180	£9,360	Profit on 1,550	£4,024	16	0
Stamps on advᵗⁿᵗˢ in-		Profits on adᵗⁿᵗˢ in-			
creased 1/3 · · · ·	1,800	creased 1/3 · ·	9,000	0	0
	———	Profit on *Ship*			
	£11,160	*Gazette* · · · ·	450	0	0
			13,474	16	0
			11,160	0	0
			£2,314	16	0

Estimated position of the paper on the expected increase :
£2,314 16s. ÷ 52 = £44 weekly profit.

The only copy of *The Constitutional* to which I have had access is that in the newspaper-room at the British Museum. I have, however, carefully studied its pages, and here record the result of my investigations, prefacing my remarks with the statement that the facts as to the institution and progress of the journal are taken from its own advertisement columns, and may be relied upon as correct.

In the year 1836 Thackeray's stepfather, Major Carmichael Smyth, became chairman of a company called 'The Metropolitan Newspaper Company.' The capital of this company was £60,000, in six thousand shares of £10 each. The first meeting was held on the 1st August, 1836, when Major Carmichael Smyth presided, and at this and subsequent meetings it was resolved to acquire an existing journal, *The Public Ledger*, and, taking advantage of the lowering of the newspaper stamp duty, to endeavour to transform it into a political newspaper of the first rank. Accordingly, on Thursday, the 15th September, 1836, appeared No. 1 of *The Constitutional [and Public Ledger]*, which by its failure was destined to convert Thackeray from a man of fortune and *dilettante* writer for newspapers and magazines into an actual professional man of letters, and thus into one of the greatest writers of this century.

The price of this journal was 4½d. Thackeray was, from the first, its Paris correspondent. Those were stirring times in France. Thackeray seems to have thrown much energy into his work, and the importance of his letters, and of the position and type allotted to them, increased as time went on.

Considerable pains have been taken to make a complete list of Thackeray's contributions to *The Constitutional* so far as they can be identified. There is no difficulty in identifying his letters from Paris, as it is well known that Thackeray was the Paris correspondent of the journal, and that he signed his letters ' T. T.,' a signature used also by him at other times and in other papers. It is not, however, in itself a pleasant task to look through number after number of an unwieldy daily journal in search of these letters, which appeared at irregular intervals, and it may be that the following list is not absolutely complete. The dates are given in tabular form for convenience of reference :

1.	September 27th, 1836.	
2.	September 29th	,,
3.	October 5th	,,
4.	October 8th	,,
5.	October 11th	,,
6.	October 13th	,,
7.	October 14th	,,
8.	October 18th	,,
9.	October 21st	,,
10.	October 22nd	,,
11.	October 29th	,,
12.	October 31st	,,
13.	November 5th	,,
14.	November 9th	,,
15.	November 14th	,,
16.	November 16th	,,
17.	November 18th	,,

18. November 22nd, 1836.
19. November 26th   ,,
20. December 1st   ,,
21. December 8th   ,,
22. December 14th   ,,
23. December 19th   ,,
24. December 20th   ,,
25. December 22nd   ,,
26. December 23rd   ,,
27. December 26th   ,,
28. December 31st   ,,
29. January 2nd, 1837.
30. January 4th   ,,
31. January 6th   ,,
32. January 7th   ,,
33. January 10th   ,,
34. January 13th   ,,
35. January 14th   ,,
36. January 18th   ,,
37. January 19th   ,,
38. January 21st   ,,
39. January 24th   ,,
40. January 28th   ,,
41. January 31st   ,,
42. February 3rd   ,,
43. February 8th   ,,
44. February 18th   ,,

Here the Paris correspondence from ' T. T.'
comes to an end, and there seems to be little room
for doubt that Thackeray, as one of the principal

supporters of the paper, both with money and brains, had been summoned to London to consider how long the owners should continue to issue the journal, and also some contemplated changes in its form.

In February, 1837, editorial announcements were made that *The Constitutional* would be enlarged on the 1st of March to a size 'exceeding that of any other daily journal.' And on March 1st it duly appeared with an additional column, making seven columns in all, on each of its four pages.

From this time one observes, on glancing through the paper, a great increase in the number of the reviews and literary and art notes, and it seems probable that Thackeray was then working regularly for the paper, and making use of the experience gained by him in the conduct of *The National Standard.* These are, however, mere speculations, and it only remains to tell in a few words the story of the remaining days of the ill-fated *Constitutional.*

In March, 1837, ominous announcements were made to the shareholders of a further call of £1 per share, making a total of £7 per share paid up. On the 10th May, 1837, notice was given of an adjourned meeting of the shareholders of the Metropolitan Newspaper Company to be held on the 13th May. The result of this meeting may be seen in the reduction of the size of each page of the paper to the original six columns, which took place on the 5th June, the price remaining five-pence.

On the 22nd June *The Constitutional* appeared in mourning for the death of the King, and in anticipation, perhaps, of its own impending dissolution. Indeed, on the 1st July it appeared for the last time with a farewell address, which, it has been suggested, may have been written by Thackeray himself, the last words of which it is interesting, especially at this period of the Queen's reign, to note, were: ' Our best [? last] wishes may be comprised in two cordial ones: To the young Queen, a long reign and a merry one; to the people, the Franchise, with Lord Durham for a minister.'

Thus ended *The Constitutional,* which is entitled to be gratefully remembered as having probably been the immediate means of transforming William Makepeace Thackeray from an amateur in literary and artistic work into an earnest professional author, whose works rank, and will continue to rank, as second to none of the great literary products of the reign which was then just beginning, and has now completed its fiftieth year.

That *The Constitutional* was by no means a contemptible, though an unsuccessful journal, and that Thackeray had no reason to be ashamed of his connection with it, may be gathered from the fact that its supporters included such men as George Evans, William Ewart, George Grote, Joseph Hume, William Molesworth, John Arthur Roebuck, Edmond Beales, and many other noted Liberals and Reformers. Its *raison d'être* may be said to have been advocacy of the ballot.

It is worthy of notice that even this second journalistic disaster did not cure Thackeray of his wish to invest money in periodicals, as will be seen from the following letter, which he subsequently wrote to William Jerdan:

'13, Great Coram Street, Brunswick Square

'MY DEAR JERDAN,

'Is it fair to ask whether the *Literary Gazette* is for sale? I should like to treat; and thought it best to apply to the fountain-head,

'Of whom I am always,

'The obligated

'W. M. THACKERAY.'

It may be assumed that this negotiation led to no result.

SKETCH FOR 'MRS. PERKINS'S BALL.'

CHAPTER IV.

No task is more difficult for the Thackeray bibliographer than that of identifying his author's early contributions to *Fraser's Magazine*. That this statement is not made lightly, or without good reason, will appear from a consideration of the following facts.

Thackeray was acquainted with *Fraser's Magazine* from the beginning. This is shown by his reference to it in the extract here given from a letter which he wrote to Mr. G. H. Lewes on the 28th April, 1855, with regard to Goethe: 'Any of us who had books or magazines from England sent them to him, and he examined them eagerly. *Fraser's Magazine* had lately come out, and I remember he was interested in those admirable outline portraits which appeared for a while in its pages.' Again, Thackeray's portrait appears, in a conspicuous position, in Maclise's group of the contributors to *Fraser's Magazine*, which was issued with the number for January, 1835, so that it must be assumed that he was then at least an occasional contributor to its pages; yet there has been no completely satisfactory evidence as to Thackeray's authorship of any paper appearing in *Fraser's Magazine* before November, 1837, when the first instalment of 'The Yellowplush Correspondence' was published. In writing thus the strong support given by such men as Dr. John Brown and Mr. A. C. Swinburne to the theory that Thackeray was the author of 'Elizabeth Brownrigge,' which was published in August and September, 1832, is not forgotten ; but after most careful consideration of all they have written on the subject, and of the story itself, it seems to be impossible to concede to 'Elizabeth Brownrigge' the honour of counting Thackeray as its author.

It was at first hoped that the books relating to the early days of *Fraser's Magazine* might be available as evidence on this interesting subject, but Messrs. Longmans, Green, and Co. write that 'the books referring to *Fraser's Magazine* so far back as 1834 and thereabouts are no longer in existence.' There are, it is believed, no surviving contemporary relations of Thackeray who could be applied to for information, and as we are considering writings of a period more than fifty years ago, we cannot expect to find many people of any kind now alive who were then old enough to be concerned in literary matters. Unfortunately the surviving contemporary relations of Mr. James Fraser, with every inclination to assist in my researches, have been unable to help, as they were too young at the period in question to have known anything of the working of the magazine. Thus it will be seen that all certain means of know-ledge have failed, and we are consequently thrown back upon deduction and conjecture with reference to Thackeray's early anonymous contributions to *Fraser's Magazine.* With the object of identifying some of these early writings, I have laboriously read through the early volumes of the magazine, extracting all papers which, from their subject or style, suggested any probability of their having been written by Thackeray. The pieces so selected have been carefully read through again and again, seeking for any expression or reference which might serve to strengthen or weaken their claims, and in this task of selection I have had the assistance of others well qualified and entitled to express an opinion on the subject; yet after all I have only been able conclusively to identify one solitary ballad, though there are many pieces both in prose and verse that may have been, and probably were written by Thackeray.

The ballad referred to appeared among the *Fraser Papers* for May, 1834, and as it was considerably altered before its reappearance, and has the interest of being Thackeray's earliest recognised contribution to the magazine, it is here reprinted with the Editor's remarks:

'And yet we need not quit French song-writing, for here's an imitation of Béranger's first song, the 'Roi d'Yvetot,' a glorious chant it is, and, we presume, utterly untranslatable; but 'The King of Brentford' is by no means to be despised.'

> '*Il était un Roi d'Yvetot.*'—BÉRANGER.
>
> 'There was a King in Brentford,
>   Of whom no legends tell,
> But who without his glory
>   Could sleep and eat right well.
> His Polly's cotton night-cap,
>   It was his crown of state;
> He loved to sleep full early,
>   And rise again full late.

'All in a fine straw Castle
    He eat his four good meals,
And for a guard of honour
    A dog ran at his heels ;
Sometimes to view his kingdoms
    Rode forth this monarch good,
And then a prancing Jackass
    He royally bestrode.

' There were no evil habits
    With which this king was curst,
Except (and where's the harm on't ?)
    A somewhat lively thirst.
And subjects must have taxes,
    And monarchs must have sport ;
So out of every hogshead
    His grace he kept a quart.

' He pleased the fine Court ladies
    With manners soft and bland ;
They named him, with good reason,
    The Father of the Land.
Four times a year his armies,
    To battle forth did go ;
But their enemies were targets,
    Their bullets they were tow.

' He vexed no quiet neighbour,
    No bootless conquest made,
But by the laws of pleasure
    His peaceful realm he swayed ;
And in the years he reigned
    Through all his kingdom wide,
There was no cause for weeping,
    Save when the good man died.

' Long time the Brentford nation
   Their monarch did deplore—
His portrait yet is swinging
   Beside an alehouse door ;
And topers tender-hearted,
   Regard that honest phiz,
And envy times departed
   That knew no reign like his.'

There are other ballads in the magazine about this
time that may have come from the same source, and
other imitations of Béranger were promised, but
certainty as to their authorship cannot be arrived at.
My remarks here, then, must take the form of queries
rather than of notes.

Passing by such seductive, but impossible, items
as ' Scenes in the Law Courts,' published in October,
1831, and actually signed ' Θ,' and ' Elizabeth Brownrigge,' of which enough has recently been written,
nothing with special claims to notice is found before
March, 1834, when there is a review called ' Hints
for a History of Highwaymen.' Again, in April,
1834, there is a long review of ' A Dozen of Novels,'
and in June, 1834, a review of ' Rookwood,' called
' High-ways and Low-ways ; or, Ainsworth's Dic-
tionary, with Notes by Turpin.' All or any of these
may have been by Thackeray. After them there is
nothing calling for mention before the article on
' Paris and the Parisians, in 1835,' which was printed
in the number for February, 1836. The title of
' The Jew of York ' (September, 1836) suggests the
author of ' Rebecca and Rowena ' ; and it seems not
improbable that he who reviewed Grant's ' Paris and
its People ' in December, 1843, may have previously
reviewed the same author's ' Great Metropolis ' in

December, 1836. There is much in the style as well as in the title and subject of ' Another Caw from the Rookwood: Turpin Out Again' (April, 1836), to suggest that Thackeray was the writer; while it is the subject and a reference to Lord Tennyson's ' Timbuctoo,' rather than any internal evidence, that suggest that Thackeray may possibly have had a hand in the ' Letters from Cambridge to Oliver Yorke, about the Art of Plucking,' etc., which made their appearance in June, July, and August, 1837. The review which appeared in April, 1837, ' One or Two Words on One or Two Books,' also, might well have owned Thackeray as its author.

Other papers of this period may suggest themselves to this or that taste as having been written by our author (the list given of possible contributions makes no pretension to completeness), but it must be remembered that in the years 1836 and 1837 he was, as has been shown in the last chapter, occupied in work for *The Constitutional*, and he may consequently not have written much for *Fraser's Magazine*.

These are, however, at best but speculations, and are put forward merely as suggestions or queries which may, though I fear they will not, lead to something more decided. The well-known ' Yellowplush Correspondence ' having once begun, we find ourselves on firmer ground. It is not proposed to refer to these or other well-known writings of Thackeray, but to mention several papers not hitherto identified which were unquestionably his work.

Before leaving ' Yellowplush ' it should be mentioned that in the ' Preface to our Second Decade,' in the number for January, 1840, appear on p. 21 these words : ' Yellowplush, with pen and pencil, contributed to " the harmless mirth of nations " ; '

while on the following page, in a description of the plate of the Fraserians, we read : ' Those who appear only in this group are . . . Thackeray, William M. In all probability comparatively few people at this time knew who ' Thackeray, William M.' was, or identified him with any of his anonymous and pseudonymous writings in *Fraser's Magazine.* By means of our friend Yellowplush we are able to ascribe to Thackeray, with what amounts to absolute certainty, some papers not hitherto recognised as his work.

The first of these is ' A Word on the Annuals,' published in December, 1837, during which month, it will be observed, there is a hiatus in ' The Yellowplush Correspondence.' On p. 760 we find this note, which shows clearly who wrote the article :

' Our friend Mr. Yellowplush has made inquiries as to the authorship of this tale, and his report is that it is universally ascribed in the higher circles to Miss Howell-and-James.'

In a note-book of Thackeray is this entry, dated January, 1838 : ' Twenty-four pages in *Fraser*, Yellowplush, Trollope, Bulwer, Landon, and a design.' In January, 1838, an instalment of ' The Yellowplush Correspondence ' appeared, as did also a long article on ' Our Batch of Novels for Christmas, 1837.' This article alone fills about twenty-four pages, so that it seemed at first that the entry was inaccurate. But on investigation it will be found that there were nearly twelve pages of ' The Yellowplush Correspondence,' and that the reviews of Mrs. Trollope's *The Vicar of Wrexhill*, of Bulwer's *Ernest Maltravers*, and of Miss Landon's *Ethel Churchill*, fill a little over twelve pages more, making together the twenty-four pages mentioned in the diary. It is clear, then, that these three reviews were written by Thackeray, the remaining notices being probably supplied by another writer.

An entry under January 4, 1838, 'Wrote a little Etiquette and read Life of George IV.,' I have not succeeded in unravelling, but another hint is given twice, first as, 'January 31. Wrote on Penny Newspapers for *Fraser*,' and again as, 'Wrote for *Fraser* on the Penny Press and Yellowplush, No. IV.—7 Feb^y.' These notes clearly identify an article in the number for February, 1838, called 'Half a Crown's Worth of Cheap Knowledge,' as Thackeray's. It deals with fifteen of the penny and twopenny periodicals of the day, among others with '*Oliver Twiss. By Bos.* 1d. E. Lloyd, Bloomsbury.' All Thackeray's generous references to his great contemporary are interesting, and the following passage is quoted as evidence of the genuineness of his admiration of Dickens's writings, shown in an anonymous and unacknowledged review :

'We come next to *Oliver Twiss*, by *Bos;* a kind of silly copy of Boz's admirable tale. We have not, we confess, been able to read through *Oliver Twiss.* The only amusing point of it is an advertisement by the publisher, calling upon the public to buy " Lloyd's Edition of *Oliver Twiss*, by Bos," it being the *only genuine one.* By which we learn, that there are thieves, and other thieves who steal from the first thieves; even as it is said, about that exiguous beast the flea there be other fleas, which annoy the original animal.'

The next entry in the note-book as to *Fraser's*

Magazine is : ' Yellowplush in April. Letter from Paris.' This is puzzling. Yellowplush is in the April number, but the only thing at all answering the description of ' Letter from Paris ' is the first of a series of three long papers called ' Our Club at Paris,' the second and third papers appearing in the numbers for May and June, 1838, and it is not probable that these were written by Thackeray.

The diary gives no more information as to contributions to *Fraser's Magazine*, but it appears from it that early in 1838 Thackeray was writing for *Galignani*, and to a considerable extent for *The Times*. These *Times* articles are dealt with in the next chapter.

In *Fraser's Magazine* for October and November, 1838, is a humorous, quizzing review of what the writer calls ' Lady Carry-the-Candle's Diary,' under the guise of ' Passages from the Diary of the late Dolly Duster, with Elucidations, Notes, etc., by various Eds.' One of the editors signs himself ' Knarf,' which, it will be seen, introduces us to another of Thackeray's numerous *noms de guerre*.

The second part of the paper begins with the following ' Note by Ed. No. 3 ' :

' *October* 25, 1838.

' With some surprise and much apprehension, I have just read the following letter (written on the back of a "weekly despatch " to Lord Yellowbelly). I at once lay it before the reader, merely noticing that, as its date implies, it was begun on the 5th, and appears to have cost the author twenty days' work to finish. Its " cacographical " purity, however, accounts for this labour.

' " *To the Editor of Fraser's Magazine.*

' " Reform Club, *October* 5.

' " SIR,—

' " A lady by the name of Duster has, I perceive, commenced the publication of her Memoirs in your Magazine. I very seldom read that miscellany, much more write in it ; and must confess an extreme disgust at a report which has gone abroad that I myself am connected in any way with the memoirs in question.

' " May I request, sir, that you will contradict this rumour, which is likely seriously to injure me in the Society in which I have at present the honour to move. A member of the Club from which I address you this note, a partisan (as far as my efforts go) of ministers, a friend of the most celebrated literary men in England, it would ill become me to contribute to a miscellany like yours, or to attempt by a stupid series of cacographical errors to awaken the laughter of the public. A gentleman, sir, should never be a buffoon ; it is a poor wit which is obliged to adopt such vulgar means for obtaining applause. In case you refuse the insertion of this letter, I need not say that I shall expect *a very different species of satisfaction.*

' " I have the honour to remain, Sir,

' " Your obedient servant,

' " FITZROY YELLOWPLUSH.

' " P.S. (*Private.*) Haven't I got on in spelling ? Come and dine here some day : we let people in while the Irish members are out of town. I have got a novel in the style of a certain friend of mine, for which I want to make arrangements with you : it's got poetry, classix, metafizzix, and is crammed chock full of bits of Greek play. Do you twig?"'

It is certain that no writer among *Fraser's* staff other than the author of 'The Yellowplush Correspondence' would have referred in such terms to 'cacographical errors,' and it will hardly be doubted that 'Dolly Duster' is to be added to our list of Thackeray's contributions to *Fraser's Magazine.* It is unquestionable that there must be many other unrecognised papers by Thackeray in the magazine, such as 'Paris Pastimes for the Month of May' (June, 1839), 'The Paris Rebels of the Twelfth of May' (August, 1839), and 'The Fêtes of July' (September, 1839); but it is difficult to positively identify any others about this date as his work.

I think, however, that I may claim that, apart from suggestions or queries, the labours of the future bibliographer have been lightened by showing beyond dispute that several of the unclaimed contributions to *Fraser's Magazine* owed their existence to Thackeray.

CHAPTER V.

THE nature and extent of Thackeray's early writings for *The Times* have always puzzled those who have written on the subject.

Anthony Trollope, in his monograph on Thackeray in the *English Men of Letters* series, wrote, p. 14 : 'For a while he was connected with *The Times* newspaper, though his work there did not, I think, amount to much.'

Mr. James Hannay, in his *Memoir*, p. 14, says : 'He certainly contributed something to *The Times* during Barnes' editorship, an article on Fielding amongst them ; though not, we should think, leading articles—a kind of work for which he had no relish, and for which he believed himself to have no turn.'

A gentleman whose knowledge should be second to none on the subject writes : 'Thackeray's connection with *The Times* was before my time and before Delane's time, if it ever existed. I have heard a rumour to that effect and that is all.'

It will be seen from these quotations that not much is actually known on the subject. Some

My dear Miss Laura

Words quite fail me. I never saw such a beautiful pen
wiper in my life. Receive in lieu of it the thanks and
blessings of an old man.—

light has, however, lately come from the publication
of letters and otherwise. It was from a letter of
Carlyle that Thackeray was identified as the author
of the review of Carlyle's *French Revolution*, which
appeared in *The Times* on Thursday, August 3,
1837, p. 6, cols. 4-6. The article on Fielding
mentioned by Mr. Hannay was referred to in one
of Thackeray's own letters to Mrs. Brookfield, which
appeared in *Scribner's Magazine* for July, 1887; and
Mr. Blanchard Jerrold, in his *Life of George Cruikshank*, has named Thackeray as the writer of the
notice of Cruikshank's Gallery printed in *The Times*
on Friday, May 15, 1863.

I believe, however, that these articles have been
looked upon as probably comprising most, if not all,
of Thackeray's writings for our leading journal; but
this is, as will be seen, by no means the case. It
will be remembered that Mr. James T. Fields, in
his *Yesterdays with Authors*, p. 27, has quoted the
following saying of Thackeray, as to the date of which
we are only told that it was some time after the
publication of *Vanity Fair* :

' " I turned off far better things then than I do now,"
said he, "and I wanted money sadly . . . but how
little I got for my work! It makes me laugh," he
continued, " at what *The Times* pays me now, when
I think of the old days, and how much better I wrote
for them then, and got a shilling where I now get
ten.'

It is doubtful, however, whether, with the excep-
tion of the isolated article on Cruikshank's pictures
above referred to, Thackeray wrote much for *The
Times* after the Review of ' The Kickleburys on the
Rhine,' and his reply to that Review, though it is

quite certain that in his early days he did write
regularly for the paper; as Mr. Hannay says, not
leading articles, but reviews of books, and in all probability also notices of pictures and perhaps of plays.

In Thackeray's note-book, referred to before, occur
many entries, at the end of 1837 and the beginning
of 1838, of receipts from *The Times;* and I have succeeded, with much search, in identifying without
doubt several articles, briefly referred to in this note-
book, of which it is proposed to give some account.
Closely following, 'Sent to *The Times* my acc' for
10½ cols.,' comes, 'Wrote Marlborough—2.' A diligent search in the files of the journal has resulted,
with the help of this hint, in discovering in *The Times*
for Saturday, January 6, 1838, p. 6, cols. 4-6, a review on the 'Duchess of Marlborough's Private Correspondence.' This article begins with the following
characteristic passage :

'The dignity of history sadly diminishes as we
grow better acquainted with the materials which
compose it. In our orthodox history-books the
characters move on as in a gaudy play-house pro-
cession, a glittering pageant of kings, and warriors,
and stately ladies, majestically appearing and passing
away. Only he who sits very near the stage can dis-
cover of what stuff the spectacle is made. The kings
are poor creatures, taken from the dregs of the company; the noble knights are dirty dwarfs in tinfoil;
the fair ladies are painted hags with cracked feathers
and soiled trains. One wonders how gas and dis-
tance could ever have rendered them so bewitching.
The perusal of letters like these produces a very
similar disenchantment, and the great historical
figures dwindle down into the common proportions

as we come to view them so closely. Kings, ministers
and generals form the principal *dramatis personæ* ;
and if we may pursue the stage parallel a little
further, eye never lighted upon a troop more contemptible. Mighty political changes had been worked
in the country, others threatened it equally great.
Great questions were agitated—whether the Pro-
testant religion should be the dominant creed of the
State, and the Elector of Hanover a King, or whether
Papacy should be restored, and James III. placed on
the throne—whether the continental despotism aimed
at by Louis should be established, or the war continued to maintain the balance of power in Europe,
or at least to assure the ascendancy of England—on
these points our letter-writers hardly deign to say a
word. The political question seems only to be used
as an engine for the abuse of the opposite party.
The main point is whether Harley shall be in or
Godolphin, how Mrs. Masham, the chambermaid,
can be checked or won over, how the Duchess of
Marlborough can regain her lost influence over the
Queen, or whether the Duke is strong enough to do
without it, can force his Captain-Generalcy for life,
and compel the Queen to ensure to his daughters the
pension and places of their mother.'

The whole article, which fills upwards of two
columns, is of interest as giving Thackeray's early
views of people and things in a time upon which he
wrote much in later years, and will repay the student
who takes the trouble to look it up and read it. A
further entry in the book reads as follows : ' Wrote
Love on Wednesday night.' These few words
enabled me to fix upon two articles as having been
written by Thackeray, but identification is further

helped by another note : ' Jan. 11, 2 cols. ½ Lady C.
Bury.' In *The Times* for Thursday, January 11, 1838,
p. 3, cols. 1-3, will be found an article, or rather two
articles, headed 'Eros and Anteros, or " Love," by
Lady Charlotte Bury,' and 'A Diary relative to
George IV. and Queen Caroline.' The first begins
in a style which would rather surprise the readers of
a review in *The Times* of to-day, as follows :

'Cupid ought to have reviewed the first of these
works—*Love;* but his Lordship was engaged with
some of his *other* foreign affairs, and therefore it has
been done by divers hands. We purpose merely to
describe it. The plot of her ladyship's novel, or
rather the text on which she writes her sermon on
love, runs thus.'

A sarcastic sketch of the plot and the absurdities and
improprieties with which the story teems is then
given, and the review closes in these terms :

'Ladies may be neglected in genteel society, but
they are not often *thrashed.* Husbands may be un-
faithful, but they do not introduce mistresses to their
wives and daughters. . . . It is against this particular doctrine of Lady Charlotte Bury's that we cry
out. We are not anxious to show that the details of
her ladyship's novels are dull, and the morals faulty;
the reader can draw his own conclusion for himself.
We only beg humbly to offer the opinion that a lady,
when she is kicked by her husband, is not in duty
bound to live with him; and that when she is be-
trayed and insulted by him she is worse than a fool
to respect or to love him. In fact, the passion in
such a case is not love, but a base, degrading, pru-
rient imbecility. It is impossible, however, to say

how all this may be in exclusive society, but we may whisper that any member of such society who betrays its mode of life (if such be its mode of life) is a very silly and ridiculous person.'

The next article is a review of ' A Diary of the Times of George IV.,' which is, I venture to think, a model of outspoken, unsparing, slashing condemnation :

' We never met with a book more pernicious or more mean. It possesses that interest which the scandalous chronicles of Brantôme, and Rabutin, and the ingenious Mrs. Harriette Wilson have excited before, and is exactly of the same class. It does worse than chronicle the small beer of a Court—the materials of this book are infinitely more base ; the foul tittle-tattle of the sweepings of the Princess of Wales's bedchamber or dressing-room, her table or ante-room, the reminiscences of industrious eavesdropping, the careful records of her unguarded moments, and the publication of her confidential correspondence, are the chief foundations for this choice work.'

The writer then protests against such a book having been written by a woman, ' a woman, too, who has eaten at her table,' etc., gives reasons for ascribing the authorship to Lady Charlotte Bury, and finishes with :

' There is no need now to be loyal to your Prince, or tender of his memory. Take his bounty while living, share his purse and his table, gain his confidence, learn his secrets, flatter him, cringe to him, vow to him an unbounded fidelity, and when he is dead, *write a diary and betray him !*'

I had an easy task with the next entry, which is
' 31 January. Holt in *The Times*,' and had no difficulty in finding in the paper for January 31, 1838,
p. 2, cols. 4-5, a review on the ' Memoirs of Holt, the
Irish Rebel.' This review is mainly occupied with
extracts from the book, and presents no special points
of interest. Indeed, nothing but the extract above
quoted would have led me to attribute it to Thackeray,
and any interest it may possess it must owe simply
to its authorship. As an instance of the care be-
stowed by Thackeray upon his work, an earlier note
is quoted : ' Jan. 11, re-wrote Holt.' The last entry
to help in our quest is 'Southey, *Times*, 16 April ';
and on turning to the journal for April 17, 1838, p. 6,
cols. 4-5, the article is question is found, ' The
Poetical Works of Dr. Southey, collected by Himself,'
from which I quote the following passage, which
not only shows considerable critical acumen, but
possesses a special interest as having been written
by so introspective a man as Thackeray :

' Were we disposed to examine or account for Mr.
Southey's peculiarities as a poet, we could find no
better means of explaining them than are here given
by himself. A small and amiable coterie of partial
friends, continued solitude, a long habit of self-con-
templation, are what Mr. Southey calls the greatest
of all advantages, and what another perhaps would
declare to be amongst his greatest drawbacks. A
timid man of business cannot be other than a vain
one, and the continued study of the *ego*, thus en-
couraged by temperament, situation, and unceasing
praise of friends, cannot surely induce to the healthy
development of the poetical character. Such a man
may examine himself a vast deal too much ; in the

pursuit of this study (and a very fascinating study it
is) he forsakes others fully as noble, and quite as
requisite to complete his education as a poet. Surely
the period of solitude and contemplation should not
commence too early, for repose, which is so whole-
some after action, is only enervating without it, and
a strong genius, like a powerful body shut out from
the world and the fresh air, grows indolent and flaccid
without exercise, or, what is worse, morbid. Some
particular quality of the mind or body (especially
where there is an original tendency to disease)
becomes unduly developed and inflamed. In a poet
we may venture to say that the disease (fatally
aggravated by seclusion) is self-approbation. It is a
vital part of his mental constitution, but it requires
careful exercise, diet, medicine, else it inflames to
such an extent as to choke up all the other functions,
and colours everything with its own sickly hue. A
poet in such a condition becomes like a bilious
millionnaire from India—his wealth and all the world
are nothing to him—he can only muse and moan
over his unhappy liver. We do not mean to hint
that Mr. Southey is in any such condition . . . but
we would only say that he retired too early from the
world, where he might have found a healthier and
even higher school of poetry than in his quiet study
by his lonely Cumberland lake. A man may be an
exquisite painter, like Gerard Dow, for instance, and
give us a complete and delightful picture—of an
interior, let us suppose, with a single figure studying
—it was Dow's general subject ; but a *great* artist has
the world for his subject, and makes it his task to
portray it.'

Unfortunately the notes help in the work of identification no more; but it will be seen that at this date

—1837-38—Thackeray was doing regular work for *The Times*, and it cannot be doubted that in time other articles will be identified as his. There are several of those I came across in my search which I am practically certain were written by him; but, adhering to the rule which has throughout governed these notes, I have resisted the temptation of ascribing anything to our author on mere assumption, con‑ fining my remarks to such writings as I can prove must have come from his pen.

CHAPTER VI.

IT has frequently happened that British authors have been indebted to American readers for encouragement by recognition of their earlier works, while as yet unnoticed among their own countrymen. Even when this encouragement takes the form of simply reprinting and annexing their works, and brings them no pecuniary profit, it is encouragement for all that. As has been shown, Thackeray was actually employed to write for an American journal, and it is certain that the American reading public have from the first shown a keen appreciation of Thackeray's ability. This is shown by the numbers of collected editions of his Miscellanies which appeared in America before anybody had thought them worthy of reproduction here.

It is proposed to give short particulars of such writings of Thackeray as appeared in book form in America before they were so published here, and to note the variations between the contents of the several volumes as first published in the two countries.

In 1852 Messrs. D. Appleton and Co., of New

York, published in 'Appleton's Popular Library' a
great many of Thackeray's Miscellanies, of which
the following volumes are in my collection.

 1. *The Yellowplush Papers*, 1852. This volume has
in itself no special interest, as it was taken from the
Comic Tales and Sketches of 1841. The announce-
ment of the volume, however, mentions, after a
reference to the London edition of 1841, that 'an
imperfect collection, long since out of print, had
previously been published in Philadelphia.' It would
be very interesting to have particulars of this Philadelphia edition, as it was probably the first volume
of Thackeray's writings published in America.

 2. *The Confessions of Fitz-Boodle; and Some Passages
in the Life of Major Gahagan*, 1852. This is remarkable as containing the third of Fitz-Boodle's 'Confessions' (which has never been reprinted in England
since its first appearance in *Fraser's Magazine*), as
well as the stories of 'Dorothea,' 'Ottilia,' and 'Miss
Löwe,' none of which were included in the English
edition of 1857, the last-mentioned having been reprinted here for the first time in the volumes of *Miscellaneous Essays, Sketches, and Reviews*, published in 1885.

 3. *Men's Wives*, 1852. This is not only the first
collected edition of these papers, which originally
appeared in *Fraser's Magazine*, but the volume contains the article, 'The ——'s Wife,' which has never
been reprinted in England.

 4. *The Luck of Barry Lyndon*, 2 vols., 1852. This
is the first separate edition, the first English edition
being that of 1856.

 5. *A Shabby Genteel Story*, 1852. The first separate
edition, though it does not contain the touching note
written for the first English edition of 1857. The
other three stories in the volume, 'The Professor,'

'The Bedford Row Conspiracy,' and 'A Little Dinner at Timmins's,' had appeared here in 1841 in the *Comic Tales and Sketches.*

6. *The Book of Snobs*, 1852. This was not the first edition, one having been published here in 1848, but it included the seven suppressed articles, which were not reprinted in England until the volume of *Contributions to 'Punch'* appeared in 1886.

7. *Jeames's Diary; A Legend of the Rhine; and Rebecca and Rowena*, 1853. The first two stories were collected in this volume for the first time, but *Rebecca and Rowena* appeared separately here in 1850.

8. *Punch's Prize Novelists; The Fat Contributor; and Travels in London*, 1853. This volume contains the first collection of all these papers. Some of them were not reprinted here until the volume of *Contributions to 'Punch'* appeared, and some do not appear even in that collection.

9. *Mr. Brown's Letters to a Young Man about Town; with the Proser, and other Tales.* This volume has a special value, inasmuch as it not only is the first collection of the papers which appear in it, but contains an 'Author's Preface,' expressly written by Thackeray for the series, and also some papers which have not been reprinted here.

There may be more volumes in this series which deserve notice; but the Americans, though willing enough to buy Thackeray's books from us, are not to be induced to part with their own first editions.

An American edition of great interest is that of *The English Humourists*, which was published by Messrs. Harper and Brothers in New York in 1853, the year of its publication here, and contained Thackeray's extra lecture on 'Charity and Humour,' which was not included in the English edition, and was not printed in this country until it found a place among the *Miscellaneous Essays* in 1885.

Since Thackeray's death many volumes of his collected papers have appeared in America, the most noteworthy being, perhaps, that published by Messrs. Ticknor and Fields in 1867, under the title of *Early and Late Papers,* which shows how carefully Thackeray's early writings had been collected and stored up. It contains, among early papers, 'Memorials of Gormandizing,' 'Men and Coats,' 'Bluebeard's Ghost,' 'Dickens in France,' and others which have only lately been unearthed and reprinted in this country. Other volumes were promised by Mr. Fields, who himself edited this, but whether they appeared or not, I cannot say.

It will be seen, however, from the above notes, incomplete as they doubtless are, that many of Thackeray's writings can only be had in their first collected form by means of these American editions, while some have not even yet been reissued here, though they were known to Thackeray's Transatlantic admirers many years ago.

Elliot Stock, Paternoster Row, London.